THAT SUMMER

TANZEELA K. HASSAN

THAZBOOK PUBLICATIONS

THAT SUMMER
Copyright © 2019 by THAZBOOK
All rights reserved. Printed in Pakistan. No part of
this book may be used or reproduced in any manner
whatsoever without written permission except in the
case of brief quotations embodied in critical articles or
reviews.
This book is a work of fiction. Names, characters,
businesses, organizations, places, events and incidents
either are the product of the author's imagination or are
used fictitiously. Any resemblance to actual persons,
living or dead, events, or locales is entirely coincidental.

For information contact :
Thazbook
03333299920
E-128 BLOCK-6 PECHS, KARACHI.
www.facebook.com/thazbook1
http://www.thazbook.com

Book and Cover Design by Thazbook Designs.
ISBN-978-969-7851-02-7
This Edition: December, 2019

A PRODUCT OF:

To My Parents.

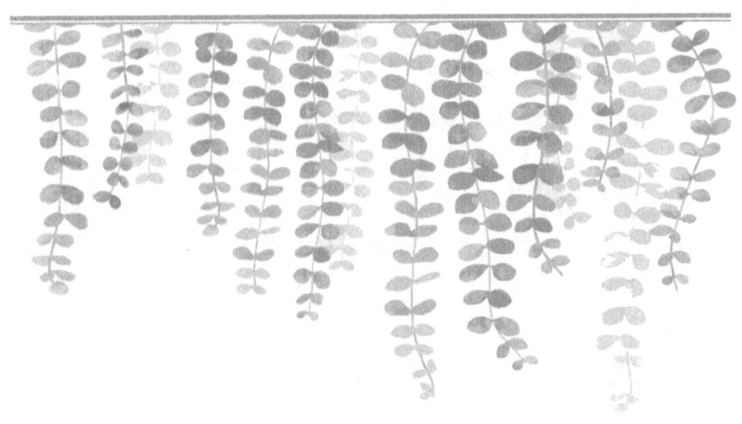

THAT SUMMER, not only did we visit our mango orchards at Mirpurkhas, but my parents decided to stay there forever. Imagine how gross! Rural life and I were two opposite things. Well, I do admit, that decision did change my life from scratch but still, I couldn't imagine why anyone would leave such a comfortable life in the city and live with those horrible smells and sounds. When you couldn't sleep after the sun hits the sky, not for a minute.

Just think about it, Me! A complete sleepyhead who always wakes up in the afternoon. How could they even think such a thing? I hadn't been sure before but then I was totally convinced that they hated me. To fan the flames of my hatred they also offered four of my cousins to stay with us until I got used to the place. How predictable. Parents never understand their kids. Why so? I don't know.

Here's the biggest example of 'never understand their kid's stuff'. They assured that if I behave and settled down nicely then we'll stay at the farms forever and if I didn't then we'll go back to the city as soon as summer ends. See? I only had to be as naughty as I could to go back to my comfy life once and for all.

Let me introduce myself formally.

Hello! I am Sumra, sixteen years old, slim and smart. Like, brainiac type of smart. Energetic and strong. Wait did I mention me being slim? Well not so slim if you relate a puffball to a wooden stick.

You can stop assuming things with me. It would never be what you think. I'm not the only child in the family. You hear me? Yes, I have the two most bothersome twin brothers and a younger sister who's the queen of annoyance.

"Have you packed yet?" That was my mother the day before we actually left the city.

"Yeah, I'm done. You know we're not going there for a lifetime, right? We'll be back after summer, so there isn't much to pack." How could I ever acknowledge that stupid decision? I simply could not.

"Excuse me? Why can't you just listen to what your parents are saying? We know what's best for you. Could you please be nice to your cousins this summer?" Ah, my Mom, always creating new topics out of the blue.

"Mama, How is my not packing related to those nieces and nephew of yours?"

"They are your cousins too dear. Please, it's my humble request. I'm sure you'll love them and the place as well. If you just open your heart for them." And she continued mixing people and places together.

"Mama, I can't find my blue upper! It was right on top of my bag last night, now it has vanished. I've searched for it the entire morning." That was Sabrina, the delightful package of shrill pitched voice. You cannot do anything but put your hands over your ears to save them from deafening.

"Oh! Dear, I folded it back into your bag this morning. Can't you just check inside your own bag before going all over the wardrobe again? I am sure you did your job well? Didn't you?" With that, the thunderstorm was over and she sped through the wooden partition to Sabrina's little room of garbage.

"Mum! Could you please tell Ahad that I'm done with him? He's so dumb! He's trying to take his X-box with him. How could he even think Baba would let him take it."

"Dear, we'll be leaving early tomorrow morning. Just be ready. Okay?" Mum replied totally overriding my request.

"Ready as always," I huffed.

"HEY! I said I'll sit by the window. Why don't you understand?" Ahad shouted at his twin.

"Hey, dude! That's my place. You know very well it's my turn today. Mama! Please tell him he sat beside the window last time." Wahid replied.

"Oh yeah? And when was that?" Ahad grabbed Wahid's shoulder and dragged him out and in no time they both were fighting and circling around the car trying to remain out of the others grasp.

"Where are we going to sit Mum? Our car is tiny and there are nine of us."

"Sarim told me that he'll be coming later. He has an important class tomorrow," said my Mum, as always giving extra information which

I don't care about.

"Still. Eight people?"

"I'll arrange something. Don't worry." Yeah, if you know what she meant.

"Here's my bag. I'll sit in the front with you Ania." Anabia informed as if I'll ever let her sit in between my parents.

"Hello Hun, that's my place." I looked at her like, duh!

"Hey, that's unfair!"

"Really? I'll tell you what's unfair. You going to our farm with us. That's unfair. This whole trip is totally unfair. So get aside will ya?" She slowly backed off.

At least she knew her place. That's my father's car. Only I was allowed to make the rules there.

"We'll have to arrange the blankets over here, that way you all could travel more comfortably," Mom said while arranging the blankets under the back seats in the space where you put your feet. She made a soft bed out of the pack of blankets. The backspace was transformed into a flat platform where the cricket team squeezed in; Ahad, Wahid, Anabia, Muneeba, Farhad and little Sabrina, all of them settled inside with crossed legs.

"All settled?" My dear father took his place with a huge sound and the car bounced up and down.

"Yes, Alhamdullillah," Mum replied but before she could complete her sentence she remembered she hadn't locked the back door to the lobby and with the lightning speed, she rushed inside the house again.

"It's amazing, right? Too good to be true." Papa was excited as a kid seeing his dream come true. He always loved to visit the farm and stay there again as he did when he was a boy himself. I seriously couldn't imagine anything amazing in that.

"Let's go." Mum came back and the journey began.

"Here, take this one. It doesn't have cheese in it." Mum insisted that I eat the sandwiches she had made. It was almost six in the morning, the sun was peeking out from behind the dry rocky hills. Everything outside was brown and muddy. I was feeling too sleepy to eat anything so early in the morning. And for that matter, the sandwiches she made! Argghhh, I would never eat that.

"Mum! Please take them away. They smell so weird," I took the lid of the box from my mother's hand and tossed it back. You must be thinking if there was anything or anyone that I love? Honestly, the word love had been erased from my dictionary ever since I was big enough to understand life. I hate it! All of it. Especially my life, surrounded by such silly people as they were.

It took us four hours to drive to our mango orchards. I slept most of the way. When our car finally took the turned onto the Mirwah

Road, the air became hotter, even though both sides of the road were embraced with thick green cultivated lands with sugar cane, wheat and cotton plants in between those huge and round mango trees.

"Ouch. Yeah, this is the place where we're going to live for the next two months" I grunted as the car navigated the muddy path that goes straight through our farms.

"Or maybe rest of your life," smirked Anabia.

After a mile's drive, we stopped near the black gate to our farmhouse. I rushed out of the car, every inch of my body was aching miserably.

"It's so hot here. I'm baked already," Muneeba said, who was the Barbie doll of our pack and one of the four cousins. She was always covered in a thick layer of makeup and no one had ever seen her with a practical hairstyle.

"Maybe try tying up your hair in a ponytail." I grabbed her silky hair and making a ponytail of it, I brushed the tips to her face and before she could retaliate, I was already far away from her, rushing inside to turn on the Air conditioning.

The house had only two rooms and a single bathroom. There was no kitchen. Just an open space by the outer wall of the house, a hand pump on the left and a stove made of bricks and wood.

The only interesting thing there was the huge Neem tree, that sheltered most of the ground by the house with a swing made out of a thick jute rope.

"Oh, Papa it's not working!" I panicked.

"What's not working?" he replied calmly placing his head over the pillow. I don't know how he does that. How could he ever feel comfortable lying over that Charpai, the most cramped thing ever used for comfort, I really have no idea.

"Papa, the AC! it's not working."

"Ah! I told Ukha to fix everything before we arrived here. Look for the socket. Maybe it's not attached?"

"It is attached, Papa. I've checked it already."

"Okay don't panic. I'll call Ukha and ask him." He simply dug his head deeper into his pillow and in no time he was snoring like a bear. Poor guy, who could blame him? he had been driving for about four hours straight.

It was almost midday and it was suffocatingly hot. To find even a modicum of relief I rushed outside. The sun was up, shining fiercely on my head and I felt the need to get away from the hustle bustle of everyone unpacking and claiming their spaces. Mama was busy setting a small kitchen out on the ground and the cousins were busy arranging bags in the corner.

I turned up my nose at such paltry tasks

and when I was about to step outside the black gate. I heard my mother asking, "Where do you think you're going?"

"Where do think I would be going?" with that I rushed out of the gate, before the rain of the questions took a turn or before someone thought I should help them with the chores. Lord above! Do they expect me to bear both chores and the filthiness of the farm together?

The heat was almost unbearable, yet I marched straight towards my love, the remains of our old Haveli. There was nothing better in this world than getting away from my family, sitting alone on those arches, and witnessing the sun as it went down. you must be thinking that it was only midday, how could I sit in one place for that long? Well, that was the magic of that place. The enchanting curves, covered in green vines surrounded by big old weeds. I could sit there for hours and hours without any food or water for I charged my energy by merely being near that sheer emptiness. The humming sound of crickets from afar and the sweet smell of flower nectar, the wildflower nectar. That place makes me feel as alive as I would ever be.

"Hey, what do you think you're doing?! Mama is calling you. She wants you to at least have something to eat before wandering off." I heard Wahid shouting from behind my back when I was halfway to my destination. I ignored him and kept walking. He added after a while, "I may remind you this is not home the refrigerator is not working so we won't be having food stocked for you to eat at odd times if you are still thinking otherwise, rush back or you'll be hungry for the rest of your day."

"ARRGGHH!!" I groaned in frustration and started to retrace my steps back to the house.

THE LIGHTS went off, making the thunderous sound of the storm more horrible. Its was a dark night and I was alone in the house. I heard the knock at our front door. For a second I thought Mama had come back home, then I realised that she can't be. She was too far away to be back so soon. I picked a bat and went out of my room, slowly, slowly; I tiptoed to the wooden door, turned the knob and...

"Boom...!"

Imagine yourself sitting between two big gravestones of your own grandparents with just one small yellow bulb hanging on a date tree at the corner, together with the soft rustling sound of leaves dancing with the wind, no other light for as far as your eyes could see and the certain knowledge that even if you were to scream, there was nobody to hear you for miles. It created a haunting ambience like no other. Then imagine being told horror stories.

Ah! I seriously loved their faces! All four of them looked like they had seen a ghost. the night was still young and we were having fun with horror stories. Or I should say, I was having fun scaring Anabia, Muneeba, Ahad, and Wahid.

They were on their toes, primed to flee, but pity, they couldn't leave without me, because the only torch we had was on my mobile and I would never let them go. I was giddy with laughter just looking at their horrified faces.

"Oh my God! You're such a monster." Wahid finally started kicking me and with him the rest of them jumped at me, trying to inflict maximum damage to make me pay for my crimes. I rolled over yet I couldn't stop laughing at them.

"Hey, guys what's going on?" suddenly, a voice from the dark inquired. I couldn't control my shriek of terror that escaped the moment I recognised the familiar call.

"Dammit, I'm dead. I totally forgot about you." I bounced back, trying to stand up and get away from the kicks and punches. Sarim our eldest cousin had arrived that evening and if I stayed there for another minute, they would reveal all the fun, I had with them and suffice to say I had to run. Run away as quickly as I could.

"Where do you think you're going? Stop right there!" Sarim Bhai ordered. No one disobeys his orders. Ever. Not even me. So I slowed my pace and stood balanced right at the tip of my toes. I didn't dare look back. I knew what was coming and the apprehension gripped me.

"Give me your mobile and stay here. I'm going to take the rest of them back to the farmhouse. Maybe this punishment would be enough for you? Could you ever for once try to be friends with your cousins? Just try to be a better part of our family?" His usual lectures continued until I couldn't hear them.

And they left me alone.

Let me give you a little more detail about my surroundings that night. I was in the middle of the remains of our old Haveli, once destroyed by floods. The graves were up on a small platform almost two feet high from the grounds, surrounded by those enchanting arches with vines and weeds. Only that, they felt enchanting in broad daylight, at night time it created the most popular scene from any horror movie and oh dear, don't forget the moving light and the tree leaves.

There was no way I could go back to our farmhouse, not without any light. It was a dark night, a pitch black one. I hate to admit but I was scared as hell.

"Dig my Grave in between these two," I shouted although they had gone far away to hear any of my calls.

This was the first time I had honestly felt the fear. The five minutes I spent there listening to the night seemed like ages. Then it all happened within a split second.

The ground started to shake, the wind blew past furiously, shaking everything with it. I rushed towards the small trunk of the date tree but I slipped before I could even reach half of the way. The vigorous movements of the ground increased. My body was rolling in between the graves of my grandparents. Suddenly the gap widened and a crack started to appear under me, out of nowhere. The last thing I remember that night was the dust and damp soil hovering over me, about to engulf me their deadly embrace.

THE FIRST thing I remember after coming back to consciousness was the humming sound of wind blowing above me. I tried to open my eyes but they were jammed, I could feel the dust caked inside my eyelid. Unintentionally, I reached out to them with my hands filled with mud, which made them worse than before. I blinked twice.

"Ugh! Dirt. Gross!" And then the realisation hit me. "I'm alive!" I exclaimed the joy that had hit me at this discovery faded soon when I realised that I was deep underground between the graves of my grandparents. One place no one would have ever want to be.

"Anyone there? Please! help me!" Terrified out of my wits, I proceeded to scream my throat out and didn't stop for a whole long hour, or maybe more. Hell, I couldn't count minutes right in the middle of a traumatic event. I don't know how long I called for help and when I was dreading being stuck there forever and that help would never come, it happened.

Someone threw down a rope made of cloth. I grabbed it and climbed up and when I could clearly see who it was, I almost jumped back to the crevice, hey, don't judge me, anyone in my place would do such. The shock was evident in my every move. I barely managed to stand on that hot sand. Yes, there was sand and rocks everywhere around me. Not a sign of the mango trees. In fact, there weren't any plants at all. Not like they were destroyed by the earthquake but the scenery ahead of me ensured that there wasn't any greenery there at all. Just desert as far as the eye could see.

Yet the shocking view was not the desert itself, but the person who had thrown the rope to me. It was a boy, wearing some kind of weird cloth. A white long unstitched piece of cloth draping over his left shoulder like the Indian women would wear the Sari dress.

"Oh my, who are you? Where am I? What in the world happened to our farm? What's this place?"

In reply to all of my inquiries, he stood there glaring at me from tip to toe. Then he reached out to poke me as if to confirm my presence. After a moment, I saw a dozen men circling around me with similar clothing and similar blank faces.

"Oh wait, what are you doing?" I jumped trying to get out of the ropes that they threw over my head. Within a second, I could feel my neck twisting and bending as the rope tightened over it. I tried to loosen the grip with my hands. Breathed hard, my eyes filled with salty water. The dizziness took over me and in no time my body hit hot sand without even feeling the heat.

THIS IS ridiculous, am I dead or something? Is this a real world? Maybe that crevice took me to some other world or maybe it's just heaven? Or hell?

Akhh how stupid I am, this can't be heaven, heaven is greener and the temperature, it's hot here. Maybe it's hell but I heard hell has fire all around it and these creatures are just human. Very simple actually. It can't be happening. Why am I tied to this stupid carriage? I sat there, hands tied behind my back, right in the centre of a flat platform attached to a huge black bull. Yes, like the one we saw in Spain and it was being carried by some small men like creatures, walking alongside, with the exact blank faces. Those things were hopeless. They just walked and walked without even uttering a single word. Believe me, I tried everything, it was a long day for me. Talking and inquiring about the place from those blank dumbos, was like, hitting your head over a stone.

The sun went down and came up again, with similar harshness than the day before. My eyes refused to close even for a little while.

"Finally, something different to see. You know I was beginning to think that I had to spend the rest of my life in this stupid carriage, watching all that endless sand, not to mention the furious heat," I called out loud. As the carriage entered through a wide red bricked street both of its sides were enriched with different kinds of shops and low buildings like only one or two stories. People fixed their gaze on me as we passed them by like I was some kind of an alien. Seriously to me, they were not less than any aliens themselves. Staring constantly with their mouths shut. No one spoke, not a single word I heard, I didn't even know which language did they speak. Most of them were men, I saw some women in miserable state occasionally. They were ragged and practically anaemic, a perfect example of a skinny body structure.

It wasn't a village that's for sure, organised and well planned yet smaller than a city of a modern age. We crossed the market and entered a large gate, the environment inside was completely different. More clean and organised. Buildings were bigger than before. Most importantly the people they look like some kind of Royals with robes and turbans on their heads. Even the women, they were dressed as princesses. For a moment I thought it's great to be here, maybe they'll start worshipping me like they do in movies but, then one of the men came near, untied the other end of the rope and dragged me towards a platform up on this highest point of the city. The minute I set my eyes on the landscape. I shrieked with terror.

"Oh my, is it Mohen Jo Daro?" the one I saw in my social studies book? This can't be true."

Utterly shocked by the view, barely noticed that they simply tied me to one of the wooden pillars. The great bath right ahead of me was similar to the one in my book but this time it was filled with water and many other wooden ornaments. There were statues everywhere. Stretching throughout the landscape.

"Maybe, I should try to undo the rope." It merely came out of my mouth and there came an unexpected visitor.

It was the boy who helped me climbed up the crevice. He just stood there staring at me.

"Hey, dude! Can you please help out? I don't know what happened but honestly, I don't belong here," I begged him but that boy didn't move, not even blink.

"Don't you think I should try going back to that crevice? Yes, I think I should do that. Maybe jumping again would take me back to my home. What do you say?"

Before I could get any response from him, not that he was going to respond. I saw four men carrying a wooden chair and that boy ran away with lightning speed.

"Offf is it all gold? How could you bear all that weight over your body? I can see the reason why you can't walk," I exclaimed to the man on that chair, I couldn't even see his face properly. Every inch of his body was filled with gold.

Not even the gold man replied to any of my queries. He glared at me with his round eyes, close enough that I smelled his pungent breath. Thank God that stupid episode didn't last long. He ordered something to his men, in a language I haven't heard before and went back. Vanished. leaving me alone again.

The sun went down, it felt colder, by every minute. It was another dark night. I urged to get back to my family. Seriously I was surprised myself that I missed them? The ones I always wanted to get away from. I was worried about what happened back there.

"Maybe they all got stuck under that stupid farmhouse building. It was barely standing and that kind of shake could knock it down easily." While I was processing these thoughts. I heard some footsteps coming towards me.

"Oh Allah, please help me" I whispered and turned around, saw a small structure rushing towards me.

It was that boy again. The Little boy with the cutest gaze one could ever imagine. Within seconds he was standing near me, undoing the rope on my hands. he sounded in a big hurry.

"What? Are you taking me somewhere else? Can you please take me to the crevice?"

He placed his index finger over my mouth. Thankfully that little gesture was enough for me to get the hint that I should be quiet.

He grabbed my hands and sped off in the opposite direction from where we came. We ran like hell. Sometimes he would stop to have a clear look ahead and then we would run like crazy. In no time we entered a large field of what looked like wheat plants to me. My feet started to hurt badly.

"I need to stop please." I barely managed to get those words out but that boy, he just grabbed my hand again and continued to run.

The sun came out and we were still running. I don't know why I followed him that night. It was his cute face or the way he did it. I never thought for a single second that running away was a bad idea.

The desert felt hotter than the day before when I was just crossing it on that wood cart.

"I said I have to stop. Okay? I have to pray." I showed him through the worst sign language that I could ever use but thankfully he understood. We stopped near a small pond in between the rocks. I washed my face and performed Wudu. I regret the times when my

Mum begged me to learn the Duas. They were the only thing I needed that day. I knew only Allah could help me get out of this nightmare.

Ten minutes of prayers in the middle of nowhere, boosted up my energy and I became fresh but that boy had a serious problem, he grabbed my hand again and started running faster than before. I don't know, what his problem was, I couldn't see anyone nor could I hear anything yet he kept on running as if he was being chased by wild dogs.

We crossed the rocky area and when we were at the mouth of the last hill, ahead of us was the desert land, the one I had travelled the day before, then, I knew he was taking me to that crevice.

"Are they waiting for us?" I inquired and as usual, he shushed me up, grabbed my arm again and ran towards our left, where there were rocky hills. Now, you must be wondering why didn't we go ahead. Would you honestly think that one would proceed towards disaster by themselves? There were at least twenty men on horseback waiting for us. The boy was more clever than I thought. He slipped through the sandy hills and we were out of their sight within minutes but we didn't stop. We ran and ran until I saw what I desperately wanted.

The Crevice.

Right in the middle of hot sand was a crack exactly the same as I had left it the day before.

"YUCK, WHY do I have to do this?" I cursed the situation I was in. I had to climb up the crevice again and this time, I didn't even have the rope that the boy had thrown back then. I grabbed the small old roots protruding from the sides of the crevice and clambered up only to find a completely different world.

There I was, in the middle of a bedroom, cold. Yes, you heard me right. My body shivered the minute I stepped up into the room. Everything was red. From the floor to the walls and in the centre stood a round bed. There was a girl prone to its centre wearing strange clothes and she jumped up at my arrival saying something in Arabic that I couldn't understand.

‘‘ماذا؟ من أنت؟ ما الذي تفعله هنا’’

"I don't know what you're talking about," I responded after— oh I don't know, how much time it took me to respond as I was busy taking in the changes. The room itself was far from anything I'd seen before, not that my past visit was anything ordinary but this was outrageous. It was huge. Plain red walls, nothing else. No windows no doors. Just that simple round bed in the centre.

"What? You can speak English? Wait till I tell Mom. This is so amazing! I thought it was only me. Ah, I'll tell Mama there are people other than me who still try to learn English. I always told her that though it is a dead language does not mean it's not interesting and useful." the girl was practically jumping up on her bed.

Her bouncing reminded me of Ahad. Oh, I really hoped he was fine. I stood there, deeply shocked, I honestly missed my brother! The very brother who had always made my life miserable.

"So, who are you exactly? Did a crevice really appear in my room out of nowhere? Is this happening for real?" She crossed the distance between us, grabbed my arm and helped me walk up to her bed.

I was scared at first because this stranger was pulling me. For all I knew, she could murder me right there and no one would ever know. Maybe that is why the room was red, to hide the blood of her victims!

"I - the... I." Nothing was coming out from my mouth. What was that place? How did I get here? These type of questions were boiling in my head.

"Okay, don't panic. Let me introduce myself first." for a second I thought, she was saying that to me but then she never stopped and kept on speaking as if it was the most important thing to do.

"My name is Aydin. I'm a teenager. Wait a second! you must be from BR? Which era are you from?" her voice was hysterical with excitement and she gripped my arm tightly in case I escaped.

Hearing her like this, my fear abated somewhat. She sounded just like some of my friends back home. She might as well be Anabia! Allah, if I ever made it back, I will never ever be awful.

"Era? What are you talking about? I'm from now! Like the present year. The one where we all are from."

"Oh dear, okay what's the year right now? And what's your name? Hmm?" She smiled at me encouragingly.

"It's Twenty Eighteen and my name is Sumra." I really thought she had gone around the bend. Who doesn't know the current year?

"Ah, nice name and I love that century! I always enjoy reading stories of that time. Have you read Stephen King? Lee child maybe?"

"Yes... but who are you please tell me this is Mirpurkhas. I badly wanted to go back home." Century? Maybe I had gone into the future instead of my own time.

"Yeah— yeah eventually you will. I hope. Don't worry, everything will be okay."

"What do you mean? I want to go home now." I pressed my empty tummy unintentionally.

"Well, it's complicated. You seem like you haven't eaten for a long time now. Do you want something to eat?"

"Last time I remember it was at least two days ago that I placed any food in my mouth. Oh— I don't know what I'm talking about. Is this future or the past? Because I was in Mohen Jo Daro a few minutes ago and a boy who never said a word helped me jump back into this crevice and now I don't know what this place is. Please, help me. I'm so worried, I wouldn't be able to eat even though I'm hungry as hell."

"Girl, calm down okay. You are way in future. Years after the return of Hazrat Isa. Now could you please let me serve you any food?"

"Okay." I was totally dumbstruck with the news. I heard her mumbling some words and the room turned itself into a living area which reminded me of an old British private parlour that I had seen in a movie. Beautiful floral paintings emerged on the wall from nowhere. Some windows and a door popped up. The bed turned itself into a coffee table and two carved wooden coffee chairs came from within the walls and made their way to the table.

"Hey, surprised?" I nodded, unable to speak at the display. " Well, that red room was my theatre. I was watching animal planet. Now don't start asking how can I watch a show from your times. Remember? I love that era very much, innovative and productive. I enjoy everything except all that killing stuff of course."

She turned and whispered something again. A red light appeared from the corner of the room which turned itself into a lady wearing a red robe. Aydin gave that lady some directions in Arabic or maybe just requested her. The holographic lady produced two trays filled with food and drinks.

"Oh, I don't think I can eat that, they don't seem halal to me." The food in front of me was very inviting, colourful. My tummy started rumbling with the smell yet I knew, I had to find something Halal to eat. I was sure that the girl can't be a Muslim.

"What's halal? Oh, as in, the food that is allowed in Islam? Dear, we all are Muslims here. There are no other beliefs left in this world. Each and every being in this world is a Muslim. Everyone follows the Prophet Isa and the rules of Islam. Alhamdullillah."

"Really? You don't look like Muslim to me."

"Why So? Because I wear this dress?

Or because my hair is red?" She glared while twirling her long red dress.

"Well yes, maybe that. Hey! Are you talking about the prophecy of Prophet Mohammed? Like the one in which he said that after Esa comes back, all the humans will Start following him and become Muslim? " I inquired.

"Yes dear, it's exactly like it. Now, will you please start eating?"

I don't really know how the food tasted as I just scarfed it down until my tummy was full to bursting. Now I could concentrate on something other than my hunger, my mind started working and I became desperate to get the answers.

"How do you know that I was from the past? Like I am from your past, right?"

"Interesting question, you know there was this guy who came from 1985 AD. I heard his crevice was near Kolachi, oh I mean Karachi of your times. They researched over him for years. This crevice that he came from was his own. No one can use that tier but him. Tell me when the earthquake came you were alone around the area of this crevice right?"

"Yes"

"Then this is your own crevice tier."

"Just cut the long talk. Tell me how can I go back."

"Okay. When did the earthquake happen I mean the day and the time?"

"It was Friday night."

"Hmm, then you have to wait for the next Friday night to go back to your own time. It's Monday night today so, you have four days and three nights here."

"That's insane. How did I end up here? When it first happened, that crevice took me to the time of Moen Jo Daro and then I'm here. How do you explain that?"

"A tier works on a time span. If you go back through it before the time of its birth, you'll end up going somewhere else be it past or future. You should've waited for the next Friday night then only the crevice would take you to your own time."

"This is still unbelievable. Is this Mirpurkhas?"

"Yes, it's the same place. Tiers don't change their location yet now we call it Hayabad. This is a big city now, but we live near the fields, maybe tomorrow I'll take you out. It's merged into Hyderabad of your times."

"Oh"

"I think you should take a shower and get some sleep now. In the meantime, I'll go tell Mama that my friend from Karachi is visiting. Did I mention we do our breakfast together? And please don't go telling everybody that you're from BR okay? " with those words she left me, rushed back again and said.

"Washroom is that way."

"I can't see any door."

"Just go to your right side of the wall and

say, "غرفة الغسيل"

I did, as I was told and right in front of me appeared a glass door. I went in, the door became opaque again. I was surprised to see that the washroom was empty, there were nothing just bare walls. I tried to rush back but then I realised that maybe I should call out again.

"غسل"

And the place was embraced with everything that the modern bathing would require. As soon as I was done taking a bath, the weariness with the burden of being awake all this time overtook me, which could easily be pulled off as me being a walking zombie, dead on the inside but subconsciously awake.

HEY, GIRL it's past Tahajjud, at least wake up now and offer Fajr prayer. We all are waiting for you."

"Awe what? Fajr?"

"Yes, come offer in Jamaat with us." I opened my eyes and saw Aydin all covered up in some kind of Abaya that had a scarf within itself. She produced one for me.

"Here, perform the Wudu and please be out in the living area soon." She rushed out leaving me alone in the room. When I followed her out of the room, a wave of thunder came through my body. The living room was filled with ladies and girls, running here and there. Chattering their tongues off.

"Assalamualaikum! You Sumra? Right?"

The lady was wearing the exact full-length dress as I saw Aydin a while back.

"Yes."

"وشاح للصلاة"

She made some signs that I didn't understand the meaning of.

"She's asking about this." Aydin handed me the gown with a scarf attached to it.

"Oh, I forgot, thanks." Thankfully that piece of cloth had a stitched scarf and I didn't have to set it up myself, I just slipped it over my body.

"We are starting the Iqamah, please hurry up."

The Salah was the same as I used to pray apart from the part that they did it with Jamaat, and I could hear a male Imam's voice from nowhere. After the Salah was over everyone started greeting me, hugging and kissing my forehead.

"Let's go, I want to show you something before the sun rises completely." Aydin rushed towards another bare wall and called out something in Arabic again. A huge closet appeared with lots of Abayas and Scarves. She handed me one of my sizes. Bummer I seriously didn't know how to wear a hijab. I had never touched such a thing in my life before.

"I don't know how to put this on." she looked at me in disbelief as if I had said something she hadn't heard before.

"Really? Don't you wear this whenever

you go out?"

"Nope, never."

"Gross."

"Okay, will you please concentrate on this."

After a minute Aydin said some Arabic words again and a big door appeared right in the middle of the wall.

"Let's go."

We stepped out, the world around me was amazingly enchanting. A beautiful garden with lush green grass and trees of mangoes spreading towards the horizon, with a single paved road that went straight through the greenery. The sun was not out completely, yet the birds were singing melodiously.

"Yes, we live outside the city. Papa always loved this calm atmosphere of the fields. The city is not much far from here, only 1k meters but we enjoy being here."

"Seriously? To me, a kilometre is far too ."

"Well, we have Solarmatic Cars now. We can travel 20k kilometres in about ten minutes."

"Wow, that's awesome." By that time I became used to that kind of shocking news.

"You have a big family, don't you get annoyed by them?" I inquired after a while as we sat by the small canal. It was not like the ones we have back home., it was built up nicely with a finished cement base. The sun was gradually coming out. The yellow beans were spreading around us by and by.

"Who gets annoyed by these lovely people. I love them from the bottom of my heart."

"Okay, that's one way of thinking." I am maybe the only one in the world who does, I added in my thoughts. I don't know what happened but all this being away from my family had made me more desperate to go back.

Although I always wished it to be away from them and when it really happened, I wanted them back. Most importantly, my brothers, it seemed that I was immune to their fights and talks.

"Do you have a family? How many brothers?"

"I have two twin brothers and a younger sister."

"Wow, great. You know I don't have any brothers. Just a younger sister. She's out with Papa to attend a meeting at Bait ul Muqadas. I'm afraid you won't get to meet them."

"I still can't believe the world is free from any other beliefs? Seriously is it really true every human in this world is a Muslim now?

"Yap, that's true. We have one central governing system, every country reports to the Khalifa. And you know the literacy and the poverty rate is almost zero. We don't have many poor people to give Zakat to, no jails and the rate of crime has been down to zero as well. People don't get diseases much. Most of the people don't even know a thing about these things, I know because I enjoy reading about stuff from BR."

"What's BR?"

"Before Return of Hazrat Isa."

"Oh so.." Before I could ask anything else, a little girl came rushing said something hurriedly and left at the same speed that she came.

"Okay lovely. Let's go for our breakfast."

11 TAKE IT."

"See Mama has learned some of the words too, isn't it great." We were at the Dastarkhwan, where at least ten other ladies and girls were sitting with us, it was a mixture of Desi and Arabic food. A kind of small robot was serving the dishes throughout the Dastarkhwan.

"So what are we going to do today? Don't you go to school or something?" I asked her soon after we were back in her room.

"School? Oh, you mean Madarsa? Yes, I'm in مستوى أعلى , about to complete my first-year Madarsa ul Nabi. Hey, would you like a visit?"

"Of course, I'll be thrilled."

Honestly speaking, I was feeling changes in myself. For the first time. Could you imagine?

I never thought I could become desperate to go back to my family life. Especially when I saw the love and affection these ladies have with each other.

"I don't see any men in your family; where are they?"

"We have a separate portion for men. Every couple has two doors to their room, one that enters into the ladies living area and the other into men. Each family has a private family room which is connected to their own rooms, we enjoy our family time there."

"That's amazing, you guys follow complete Islamic pattern for living, sounds interesting."

"I still don't believe, you hadn't put on any hijab before; don't you guys follow the values of Islam?"

"Well not everyone. I am a little different, very rebellious. I never obeyed any of my Mum's requests."

"I know Islam does not order anyone by force, yet we should do what we think is best for us. All this covering makes us special"

"Yeah I know, that's exactly what my mother always told me."

"You know if you had time I would have taken you to the world tour but I've read that it's very dangerous for you and for your future if you go away from the crevice."

"Hmm, still I don't see any point in hiding the crevice from your own family. They seem nice."

"Well it's complicated in fact they'll become curious and ask you many questions and you'll get tired of answering them. The fact that you don't speak Arabic will make it worse."

"This country is still Pakistan, right? Then why do you guys speak Arabic, what happened to Urdu?"

"Well it happened after Isa's return, we, the Muslims made Arabic as a universal language of the world. It's easier that way, besides the Quran is in Arabic, we don't have many difficulties understanding it."

"Yes, that's true. I have to admit, I don't the meaning of a single Surah. That's so embarrassing."

"Really? I've read you guys had translations didn't you try them?"

"Well most of us don't bother, that's so bad, I know but it's just one of our norm."

"I don't see how any Muslim could be a good Muslim without understanding the true meaning of the Quran."

"Ah, I think I'll make a promise to you if I go back, which seems impossible, I'll make sure to learn the Arabic language or at least to read and understand the meaning of Quran."

"That would be wonderful! Hey, do you think we should watch some movies? We have these good fictional series that gives the knowledge of Quran in a fun way and besides I don't have any class until noon today. We'll go to Madarsa afterwards. What do you say?"

"Yes— a big yes."

"Okay" she turned around and ordered the holographic lady in Arabic, suddenly the room turned itself into a theatre again and within seconds the beautiful drum music started playing.

"DON'T TELL anyone that you're from the past or they'll make fun of you." We settled in a round apple shaped car, which she said, was her own obsession, they mostly had simple cars like the ones we had in the twenty-first century but she begged her father to buy her this one. It was red and round in every aspect.

"They can do that. Aren't they good Muslims?" I inquired.

"Well dear, they are kids besides everyone has a right to enjoy. It's just we have to be careful not to hurt anyone but it's really hard."

"Yes, I agree."

In no time we were in the parking lot of

her Madarsa. As we entered the premises, the view mesmerised me. Like I was being taken to a piece of heaven. The garden in the middle and the round building around it. The amazingly enchanting voice reciting the verses from the Quran.

Girls were gathering around the hall, silently taking their seats. We took ours in the back of the room. The moment we settled down. A bunch of girls came near us and started chatting with Aydin. I couldn't understand what they were talking yet I could feel, it was not pleasant.

After a while, a girl grabbed my arms and rushed towards the door we entered from. I heard Aydin calling out my name.

"Run Sumra!"

I tried to get out of her grip but she firmly gripped it, running furiously faster every moment. Out of blue came a glass door with a sign on it.

‟ناظر المدارس”

She hurried inside still grabbing my arm, soon as we entered, the lady behind the desk bounced up.

"She's from before return."

I honestly don't know what came over her, she didn't even say a single word in reply. Gripped my hand and rushed out.

//PLEASE LET me go. I have to go back to Aydin. Please don't do this to me."

It had been two days that they kept me in that small square room with no windows or door. Just a simple bunk and a washroom that appears whenever I demand. I barely touched any food that they sent with the help of small robots even though it smelled divine.

Nobody came to me, no one asked me anything. I was craving to see a human face and hear them talk.

"Please talk to me. Are you guys even listening?"

I always wanted this, being in peace and living alone was the greatest gift that I could ever get, but then after spending only three days alone, with nobody to talk to, I realized the fact that humans are a social animals, they require social life and a family structure was actually the greatest gift that one could ever have.

I was lost in my thoughts when I heard some footsteps closing by and then a whisper.

"Let's Go." Aydin emerged from behind the door and hurried towards me. I was bewitched to see the familiar face that made my day bright.

"How did you? What's this place? I honestly have to be back to the crevice." I poured out.

"Yes— yes you have to, but if you don't keep quiet, it will become hard for me to take you out from here."

"Zipped." I hugged her quickly.

We ran with softer footsteps. She kept on checking every entrance and moved on. Within minutes we were in her Solarmatic apple-shaped car.

"I don't get it. Who were those people? Didn't you say that all human beings left in this world are Muslims? I don't know why a Muslim would keep me captive like this?" I burst out, even before she started the car.

"Oh calm down, I'll tell you everything we don't have time, it's already seven o'clock in the evening and you have to be back before midnight."

"What do you mean? Isn't it Thursday? I

spent two nights there."

"Nope, three actually."

"How? I counted two."

"Cause you were knocked out in one of them."

"What do you mean knocked out?"

"Do you think they took you there for nothing?" They gave you anaesthesia before doing some tests over your body."

"Why? Aren't they Muslims?"

"Yes they are better Muslims but they take you as a threat, they think if you kept loose, here in this balanced world you could create chaos, so they tested your brain to find out your beliefs. Thank God I managed to take you out before they found out about the crevice. I had to do this, just to save you from being away from your family much longer. I'm sure they will send you back but their testing could take months or years. So thank me."

"Yes, I'm totally obliged that you helped."

"Well, maybe it's early to say so, cause I still have to take you to my room without my family noticing."

"How would you do that? Your family is big."

"Yes, I know, maybe you can squeeze into my coat? That way they won't notice."

"Great now I have to smell your sweat?"

"Ah, I don't smell so bad, you know."

I practically squeezed inside her coat and we entered her house. Thankfully nobody was there in the ladies living area or in the lobby, we finally reached the door to her room, when somebody called her from her back, she turned around, I heard her talk for a while then eventually we entered into her room.

"Oh Alhamdullillah, you can get out now."

"Jazakillah, for all this dear, what would I have done if this crevice hadn't appeared in your room and someplace else."

"Things always happens as they were meant to be and only Allah knows what's better for you."

"You know, I think you are right, hey, what do you think, can I visit you again sometime?."

"Dear, as far as I know, you can only use a tier once. Besides, how would you know when to jump to be back here?"

"That's right. Maybe things are really meant to be and you cannot play with your own life."

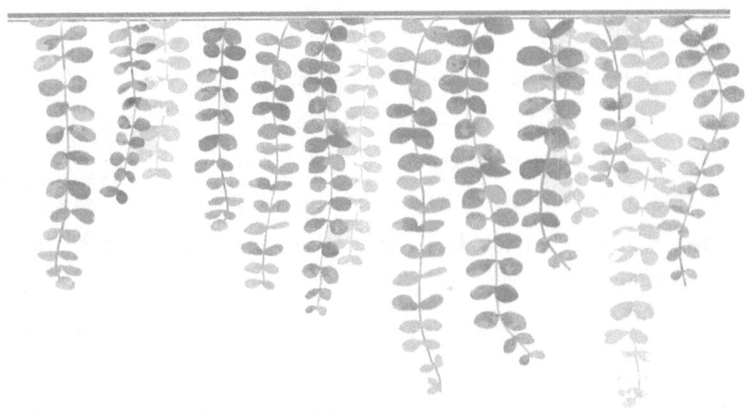

OR THE third time, I was back into the pit. Desperate to be back with my family again, yet, I didn't have any courage to climb out of the crevice, the very crevice that took me to the diverse worlds that changed my idea of living. The purpose of life had never been clearer to me before as it was after all the adventure of that summer.

Nervous as hell, I tried to grab the roots again but failed to climb up. It was night time and I couldn't see anything. All of my body jittered. I knew I had to do it, some way or the other, so I grabbed the roots again with more desperation and started my trek up to the ground but before I reached the top, the ground started to shake again more vigorously than before. I clenched the roots in my hands as tightly as I could; afraid that I would lose my hold, fall down and come back into another time. I couldn't bear it anymore. The dust settled again as I kept my place firm. Then, at that very moment, I heard the voice that I was dying to hear.

"Sumra? Are you alright? Please talk to me."

The grief in Sarim Bhai's voice told me that he had been there for a long time, asking that very question again and again. I didn't waste any second and replied.

"Sarim Bhai!! I'm fine and I'm climbing up!"

"Alhamdullillah! Allah is great!" He quickly laid against the edge of the pot to pull me out.

When I finally grabbed his hands and stepped up on the surface, a sigh of relief followed as I found myself back in between the graves and the old Haveli remains.

"Assalamualaikum, how's everyone? Please tell me are they fine? Oh, how I missed you guys!"

"Yes—yes, Sumra only you had got caught up in this earthquake, everyone else is safe and sound. I'm so sorry Sumra. I left you here. I didn't mean to leave you for this long, I was halfway back to take you to the farmhouse and that earthquake came and we couldn't find you. We thought we had lost you forever!" Sarim Bhai burst out crying like a baby.

"Bhai Sahab! Don't worry I was the bad

guy here. I'm perfectly fine Alhamdullillah. You must not worry." I smiled widely, Sarim Bhai, on the other hand, was thunderstruck, eyes fixed and mouth wide open.

"Please take me back, it's me who has to say sorry to all of my family. I need to make a fresh start. Free from mocking and full of friendly gestures. I have to learn more about Islam and Oh, most importantly I have to correct my moral and social values. I have wasted lots of my time mocking other people's life and blaming others for my actions. Now I have to be focused on myself. Once I've corrected myself, nothing can overpower me! Haven't you heard the phrase, if you want to change the world, start with yourself."

AVAILABLE AT AMAZON

HUNGER

Adam Lyons is a successful New Yorker who has never known his mother except that her life ended moments before his began. An unexpected letter from his Pakistani grandmother sends him on a quest he didn't know he needs—a path toward satisfying his spiritual hunger.

Iman, who lives on the opposite side of Central Park, could never have predicted the turns her life would take. In her search for peace, she must submit to a fate she is desperate to escape.

Max has his own plans. His entire life, he has been waiting to give them what they deserve rather than what they desire. He did it before. Now, he has to end things once and for all. His problem? He has to survive two life sentences to fulfil his hunger.

TEMOLI

Thazbook's Anthology Journal provides your tween (9-14-year olds) a creative outlet. It is a blend of both a journal and an anthology. Where we give our respected readers lessons to learn creative writing along with a treasure trove of inspirational stories written by international authors. TAJ believes in fostering the young ones to enhance their ability to write by providing them with activities and writing prompts to pour out their version.

THE VARIANT

Living down in the valley with infected plants and waiting for her brothers to bring back food from up the cliff, has always made Ayman anxious. Her urge to go up there deepened when her brothers' disappeared. Desperate to explore the world above and to look for her brothers, she sets up to the unknown world, the one they call the Metazorric Dimension.

www.thazbook.com

www.ingramcontent.com/pod-product-compliance
Lightning Source LLC
Chambersburg PA
CBHW051501140726
47987CB00006B/2829